THOMAS & FRIENDS™

Fun All Year

Illustrated by Celestino Santnach

Thomas the Tank Engine & Friends

A BRITT ALLCROFT COMPANY PRODUCTION
Based on the Railway Series by The Rev W Awdry
Copyright © Gullane (Thomas) LLC 2002
All rights reserved. Published in the United States by Random House, Inc., New York,
and simultaneously in Canada by Random House of Canada Limited, Toronto.
ISBN: 0-375-81495-7
RANDOM HOUSE and colophon are registered trademarks of Random House, Inc.
Printed in the United States of America
January 2002 10

Thomas loves the snow!

Thomas doesn't like the snow now!

Thanks, Terence!

Circle what does not belong.

skates

snowman

mittens

scarf

snowflake

hat

flip-flops

jacket

skis

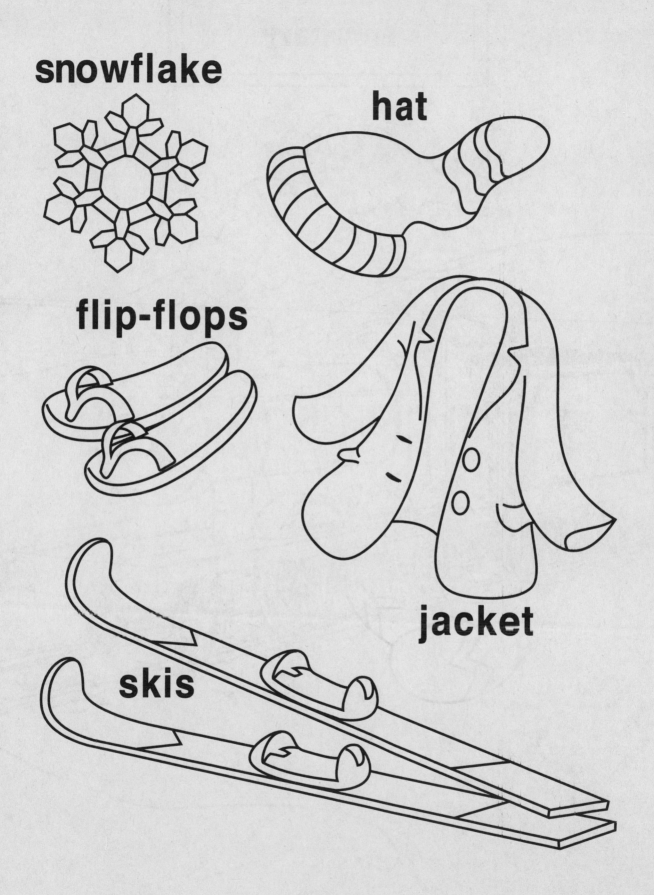

February

Will the groundhog see his shadow?

Happy Valentine's Day, Thomas!

Percy and Thomas Valentines

A great big snow train!

March

Stop that hat!

Lead Leprechaun Percy to the pot of gold!

Happy Saint Patrick's Day!

Spring is here!

Draw lines to connect the matching umbrellas.

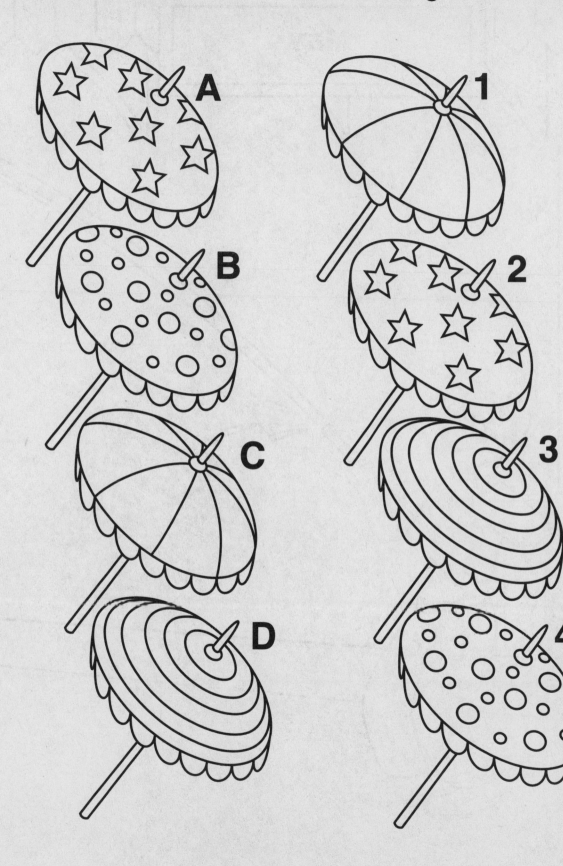

Spring cleaning.

Catch the ball, Thomas!

Thomas catches the ball!

We won the game.

Connect the dots!

What a fun picnic!

Draw something your mother loves.

June

Harold visits on the last day of school.

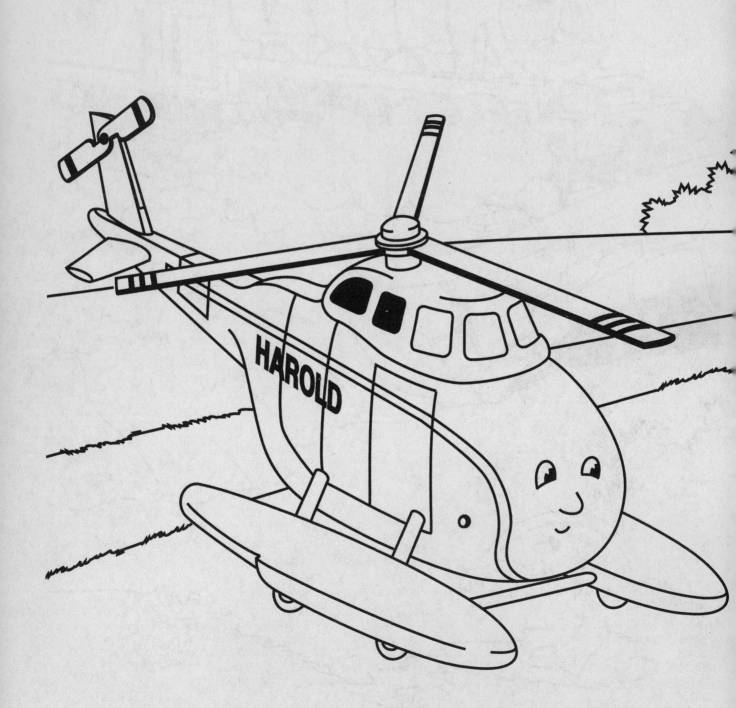

Happy Father's Day!

Today Gordon is going fishing.

July

Circle what does not belong.

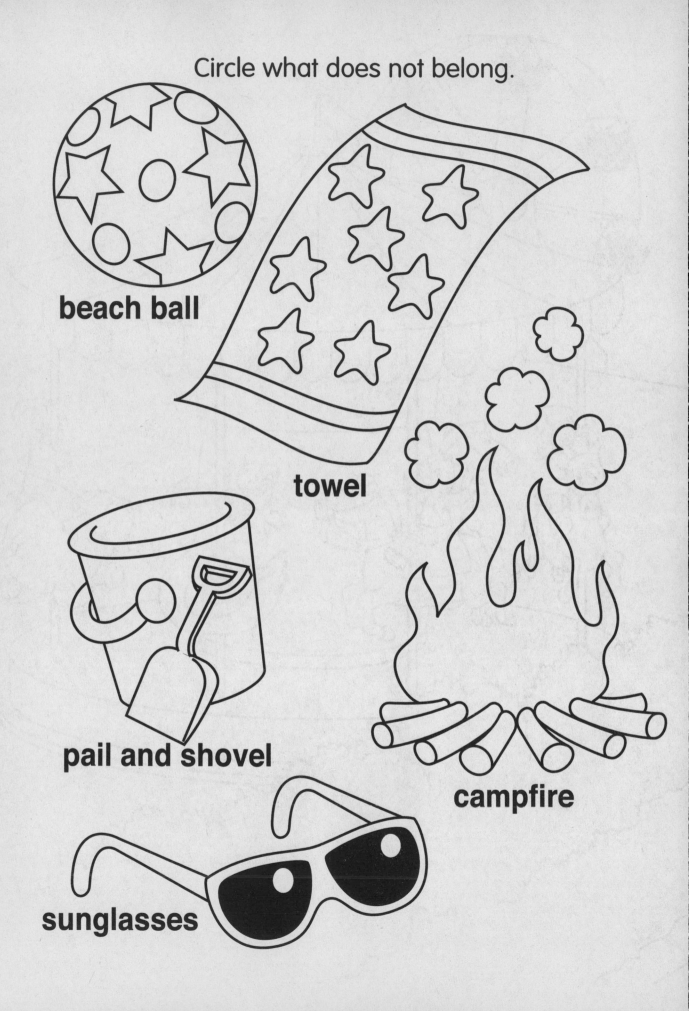

beach ball

towel

pail and shovel

campfire

sunglasses

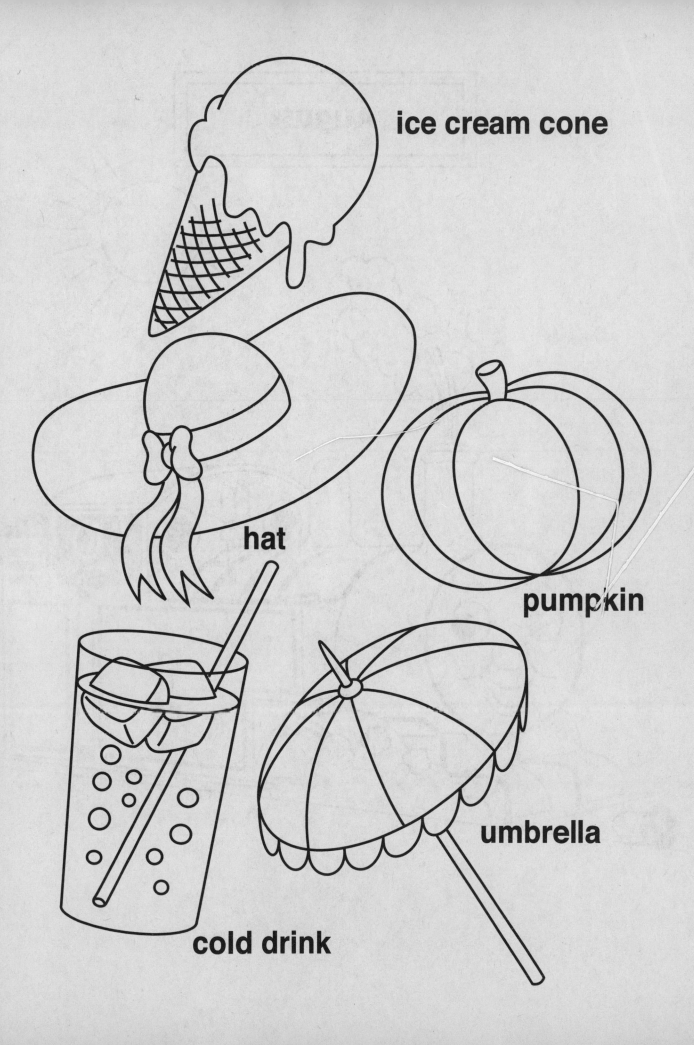

ice cream cone

hat

pumpkin

cold drink

umbrella

August

It's hot!

All aboard for the beach!

Thomas stops for a cool drink!

Home again.

September

Draw lines between the things you take to school and the backpack.

Ahoy, Thomas!

Which number goes with which engine?

1 2 3

Henry

Edward

Thomas

4 5 6

Percy

Gordon

James

Happy Halloween!

Draw a picture of something you are thankful for.

December

Happy holidays!

What a tiring year!